THE BEST JOKES FOR

11

YEAR OLD KIDS!

OVER 250 FUNNY JOKES!

With over 250 really funny,
hilarious Jokes,
The Best Jokes For 11 Year Old Kids!
promises hours of fun for
the whole family!

Includes brand new, original and
classic Jokes that will have the kids
(and adults!) in fits of laughter
in no time!

These jokes are so funny it's going
to be hard not to laugh!
Just wait until you hear the
giggles and laughter!

Books by Freddy Frost

The Best Jokes For 6 Year Old Kids
The Best Jokes For 7 Year Old Kids
The Best Jokes For 8 Year Old Kids
The Best Jokes For 9 Year Old Kids
The Best Jokes For 10 Year Old Kids
The Best Jokes For 11 Year Old Kids
The Best Jokes For 12 Year Old Kids

To see all the latest books by Freddy Frost just go to FreddyFrost.com

Contents

Funny Jokes!

Why did the giant squid eat six ships that were carrying potatoes?

Nobody can only eat one potato ship!

Why was the broom late for work at the factory?

He overswept!

Why do giraffes have such long necks?

They have very smelly feet!

What is the main difference between
a bird and a fly?
A bird can fly but a fly can't bird!

Why did everyone trust the caveman?
He was a caveman of his word!

What do you get if you cross a
boomerang with a christmas present?
A gift that returns itself!

What do you get if you cross a centipede with a parrot?
A walkie talkie!

What is an astronaut's favorite snack?
A Mars Bar!

Why was the snail so loud?
He came out of his shell!

Why were the ghosts hired
as cheerleaders?
They had so much spirit!

When the boy stayed up all night
thinking about where the sun went,
what happened next?
It finally dawned on him.

What did the hippy fisherman say
to his friend?
Keep it reel, man!

What is the key to a great space party?
Always planet early!

How does water stop flowing downhill?
It gets to the bottom!

Why did the polar bear have
a fur coat?
He lost his sweater!

What is a bird's favorite month?
Flock~Tober!

How do snowmen learn things?
They go on the winternet!

Why was the archaeologist so sad?
His career was in ruins!

What was the pirate's favorite subject at school?
Arrrrrt!

Why didn't the boy put up posters about his lost cat?
Cats can't read!

What do you call a lion that likes to wear top hats?
A dandy lion!

What kind of fish did King Arthur eat every Saturday night?
Swordfish!

What did the farmer call his cow that was twitching and twitching?
Beef Jerky!

Which elf sang the best songs?
Elf-is Presley!

What do you get if you cross a robber with a chicken?

A peck-pocket!

What do you get if you cross a toad with a galaxy?

Star Warts!

What is a puppies' favorite car?

A Land Rover!

What is the biggest ant?

An eleph-ant!

What do you do if a monster rolls
his eyes at you?

Roll them back!

What did the doctor say to the patient
who thought he was a dog?

Sit!

Which state has really small cans
of soft drink?

Mini Soda!

Why was the atom sure it lost
an electron?

It was positive!

What do you get if you cross a
monkey with a skunk?

King Pong!

What glasses do really small insects wear?

Speck-tacles!

What do you get if an elephant stands on the roof of your house?

Mushed rooms!

Which musical instrument is in your bathroom?

The tuba toothpaste!

What do snowmen sing on their birthday?

Freeze a jolly good fellow, freeze a jolly good fellow!

Why did the bacteria travel across the microscope?

So he could get to the other slide!

Why did the basketballer go to the doctor?

He had hooping cough!

Funnier Knock Knock Jokes!

Knock knock.

Who's there?

Oliver.

Oliver who?

Oliver other kids are busy so can you help me do my chores?

Knock knock.

Who's there?

Gladys.

Gladys who?

Gladys Friday!
I love the weekend!

Knock knock.

Who's there?

Yah.

Yah who?

Yahoo!
Ride 'em cowboy!

Knock knock.

Who's there?

Tyrone.

Tyrone who?

Tyrone shoe laces
lazybones!

Knock knock.

Who's there?

Weirdo.

Weirdo who?

Weirdo you want me to put your parcel, sir?
Please sign here.

Knock knock.

Who's there?

Ogre.

Ogre who?

Can you come Ogre for dinner tonight?
We're having ice cream sandwiches!

Knock knock.

Who's there?

Waiter.

Waiter who?

Waiter I tell your mom!
You're in trouble now!

Knock knock.

Who's there?

Russian.

Russian who?

I'm Russian to get to school!
Let's go!

Knock knock.

Who's there?

Scold.

Scold who?

Scold enough today to make a snowman!

Knock knock.

Who's there?

Whale.

Whale who?

Whale I'll be!
Grandma ate all the cookies!

Knock knock.

Who's there?

Harmony.

Harmony who?

Harmony times do I have to knock? Please answer the door!

Knock knock.

Who's there?

Ice cream.

Ice cream who?

Ice Cream if you don't open this door right now!

Knock knock.

Who's there?

Van.

Van who?

**Van are you going to let me in?
I'm hungry!**

Knock knock.

Who's there?

Wayne.

Wayne who?

**Wayne is coming!
I'm getting wet!
Noooo!**

Knock knock.

Who's there?

Needle.

Needle who?

**Needle hand to move your TV?
I've got big muscles!**

Knock knock.

Who's there?

Frank.

Frank who?

**Frank ly speaking I would really
like it if you fixed your doorbell!**

Knock knock.

Who's there?

Will.

Will who?

**Will you let me in before
I freeze?**

Knock knock.

Who's there?

Riot.

Riot who?

**I'm Riot on time!
Let's go!**

Knock knock.

Who's there?

Poor me.

Poor me who?

**Poor me a drink please!
I'm really thirsty!**

Knock knock.

Who's there?

Rabbit.

Rabbit who?

**Rabbit up neatly please.
It's a present!**

Knock knock.

Who's there?

Tweet.

Tweet who?

**Would you like tweet an apple?
Yummy!**

Knock knock.

Who's there?

Omar.

Omar who?

**Omar goodness, that food
smells delicious!
Can I eat it all?**

Knock knock.

Who's there?

Tank.

Tank who?

Tank goodness you finally answered the door! I need to pee!

Knock knock.

Who's there?

Voodoo.

Voodoo who?

Voodoo you think you are, making me wait so long?

Knock knock.

Who's there?

Duncan.

Duncan who?

Duncan a cookie in milk is fun! Yummy!

Knock knock.

Who's there?

Tibia.

Tibia who?

Tibia good singer you need to practice!

Laugh Out Loud Jokes!

What happened to the ghost comedian?
He was booed off stage!

What did the chewing gum say
to the shoe?
Let's stick together!

What did Mrs Claus say to Santa Claus
when she looked out the window?
It looks like rain, dear!

What did the wasp throw in the park?
A fris-bee!

Why was the oyster sad when
she left the gym?
She pulled a mussel!

Who eats at the restaurant on the
bottom of the sea?
Scuba diners!

Why did the chef spend 10 years
in jail?

**He beat the eggs and whipped
the cream!**

Why are trains good at
finishing things?

They stay on track!

How did the scientist freshen
her breath?

With experi-mints!

Why didn't the lady trust the tree?
It seemed a bit shady!

How did the horse disguise himself?
He wore camel-flage!

What sort of music does an
Egyptian Mummy listen to?
Wrap!

Which bet has never been won?
The alphabet!

What did the elephant say to her naughty children?
Tusk Tusk!

Why do only rich pirates have a hook and a peg-leg?
They cost an arm and a leg!

What did the doctor say to the lady
whose son swallowed a bullet?

Don't point him at me!

Why was the didgeridoo at the office?

**To answer the phone if
the boomerang!**

Why did the baker quit
making doughnuts?

**He was just sick of the
hole thing!**

What did the baby light bulb say
to her mommy?
I wuv you watts!

What did the lion say when it first
met the gazelle?
Pleased to eat you!

What was wrong with the sick bucket?
He looked a bit pail!

What did the doctor say to the patient
who forgot where he put
his boomerang?
**I'm sure it will come back
to you!**

Which fish has the loudest laugh?
A piran-ha-ha-ha!

Why did the dentist get promoted?
She knew the drill!

What did one elevator say to the
other elevator?

**I think I'm coming down
with something!**

Which bird steals soap from
the bathtub?

The robber duck!

What is a pig called if she can
write with both hooves?

Ham-bidextrous!

What did the dinosaur eat after his tooth was pulled out?

The dentist!

Why did the snail avoid
the drive through?

He didn't like fast food!

What do you have if you get scared by the same ghost twice?

Deja boo!

What do you call an insect who can't speak clearly?
A mumble bee!

Why did the cow go to yoga class?
To be more flexi-bull!

How did King Arthur learn to rule?
He went to knight school!

What did the tooth say to the dentist when he went to the movies?
Fill me in when you get back!

What do you do if you see a spaceman?
Park your car, man!

How can you cut a wave in half?
With a sea saw!

What car do insects drive?
A beetle!

Which dinosaur wore reading glasses?
A Tyrannosaurus Specs!

What is the best type of haircut
for a bee?
A buzz cut!

Crazy Knock Knock Jokes!

Knock knock.

Who's there?

Heaven.

Heaven who?

**Heaven seen you in ages!
How are the kids?**

Knock knock.

Who's there?

Zinc.

Zinc who?

**I zinc chocolate is tastier
than broccoli!**

Knock knock.

Who's there?

Lefty.

Lefty who?

Lefty key at home so I had to knock!

Knock knock.

Who's there?

Sonia.

Sonia who?

Sonia shoe - dog poo! Ewwww!

Knock knock.

Who's there?

Taco.

Taco who?

**I would like to taco 'bout our range of doorbells.
Do you have a spare 2 hours?**

Knock knock.

Who's there?

Chicken.

Chicken who?

**Better Chicken the oven!
Something is burning!**

Knock knock.

Who's there?

Sarah.

Sarah who?

**Sarah problem with your door?
I can't open it!**

Knock knock.

Who's there?

Wheel.

Wheel who?

**Wheel be back in 3 hours!
Please wait here!**

Knock knock.

Who's there?

Yvette.

Yvette who?

Yvette helps sick animals get better!

Knock knock.

Who's there?

Mushroom.

Mushroom who?

There wasn't mushroom at the party so I left!

Knock knock.

Who's there?

Window.

Window who?

Window we start holidays?
I think it's next week!

Knock knock.

Who's there?

X.

X who?

X on toast for breakfast?
Yummy!

Knock knock.

Who's there?

Isabel.

Isabel who?

Isabel working yet so I can stop knocking?

Knock knock.

Who's there?

Ooze.

Ooze who?

Ooze in charge of this fine hotel?

Knock knock.

Who's there?

Teresa.

Teresa who?

Teresa very green this time of year!

Knock knock.

Who's there?

Wooden.

Wooden who?

Wooden you like to let me in so I can give you your present?

Knock knock.

Who's there?

Tahiti.

Tahiti who?

Tahiti home run you need to hit the ball really hard!

Knock knock.

Who's there?

West.

West who?

If you need a West from eating your ice cream I can eat it for you!

Knock knock.

Who's there?

Paula.

Paula who?

Paula door open and you will see!

Knock knock.

Who's there?

Wendy.

Wendy who?

Wendy delivery man gets here please wake me up! Goodnight!

Knock knock.

Who's there?

Urine.

Urine who?

Urine a lot of trouble if you don't open this door!

Knock knock.

Who's there?

Wire.

Wire who?

Wire we still talking through this door?

Open up already!

Knock knock.

Who's there?

Toucan.

Toucan who?

Toucan play at that sort of game!

Knock knock.

Who's there?

Wilma.

Wilma who?

Wilma key ever work on this door?

Knock knock.

Who's there?

Izzy.

Izzy who?

**Izzy birthday party still on?
I took 4 buses to get here!**

Knock knock.

Who's there?

Walrus.

Walrus who?

Why do you walrus ask me that?

Ridiculous Jokes!

Who carries a basket, is scared of wolves and says bad words?

Little Rude Riding Hood!

Where do dogs go if they lose their tails?

A retail shop!

Why did the girl stick a hose in her brother's ear?

She wanted to brainwash him!

What did the Cinderella penguin
wear to the ball?
Glass flippers!

Why is it so cold at Christmas?
It's Decembrrrrrrrr!

Why did the locksmith have no friends?
He was too cran-key!

What happened to the cat that
ate 3 lemons?

It became a sour puss!

Why do owls love going to parties?

They are always such a hoot!

What is the best cure for dandruff?

Going bald!

What happened when the gorilla got some bad news?

He went ape!

What did the poodle say to the flea?

Stop bugging me!

What do you call a bee that's having a bad hair day?

Frisbee!

What did the magic tractor do
last Saturday?

Turned into a corn field!

What do birds send out
at Christmas?

Tweets!

Why do tigers eat raw meat?

They never learned to cook!

Why did the flea lose his job?
He wasn't up to scratch!

What do you call the hippy's wife?
Mississippi!

What do you call a zombie in a
Chinese restaurant?
The woking dead!

What did the poodle say to
his brother?

I have a bone to pick with you!

What happens if it's been raining
cats and dogs?

You might step in a poodle!

Why was the snowman lonely?

He was ice~olated!

Why did the spaceship want to play football?

So it could do a touchdown!

What would you call it if worms took over the entire world?

Global Worming!

What do you get if you cross a dinosaur with a witch?

A Tyrannosaurus Hex!

When is it bad luck if a black cat follows you?

When you are a grey mouse!

What did cavemen use to cut down trees?

A dino-saw!

Why did the iron talk to the washing straight away?

It was a pressing matter!

Where is the biggest pencil factory in the United States?
Pennsylvania!

How did the vampire race finish up?
It was neck and neck!

What do you call an ugly dinosaur?
An Eye-saur!

What Mexican food is best on
a cold day?

Brrrr-itos!

What is the busiest time to go to
the dentist?

Tooth hurty! (2.30)

In which age did Egyptian mummies
live?

The Band-age!

What did the really sleepy
man read?

The snooze paper!

What do you call a dinosaur who is
going to have a baby next week?

A Preggosaurus!

Why are tennis players so loud?

They always raise a racquet!

What did the doctor say to the patient with double vision?
Just close one eye!

Why was the cucumber sad?
She was in a pickle!

What do you call monsters who work on airplanes?
Fright attendants!

Silly Knock Knock Jokes!

Knock knock.

Who's there?

Kanye.

Kanye who?

Kanye give me a hand to lift this TV?

It's really heavy!

Knock knock.

Who's there?

Iran.

Iran who?

Iran really fast to get here and you're not even ready!

Knock knock.

Who's there?

Thor.

Thor who?

My hand is Thor from all this knocking!

Knock knock.

Who's there?

Some Bunny.

Some Bunny who?

Some Bunny has stolen my lunch!
Nooooo!

Knock knock.

Who's there?

Water.

Water who?

Water you doing later on today? Let's play some Xbox!

Knock knock.

Who's there?

Wafer.

Wafer who?

Been a Wafer for a while. How have you been?

Knock knock.

Who's there?

Henrietta.

Henrietta who?

Henrietta apple and he found half a worm!

Knock knock.

Who's there?

Watson.

Watson who?

Watson the tv tonight? I feel like watching Star Wars!

Knock knock.

Who's there?

Kent.

Kent who?

**Kent you see I want to come in?
I've been waiting for 3 hours!**

Knock knock.

Who's there?

Lettuce.

Lettuce who?

**Lettuce in please.
We are really tired!**

Knock knock.

Who's there?

Yacht.

Yacht who?

Yacht to be able to recognize me. I only saw you last week!

Knock knock.

Who's there?

Stew.

Stew who?

Stew early to go to bed! Let's play ball!

Knock knock.

Who's there?

Seymour.

Seymour who?

I Seymour when I wear my glasses!

Knock knock.

Who's there?

Thumping.

Thumping who?

Thumping brown and thlimy is crawling up your leg!

Knock knock.

Who's there?

Les.

Les who?

Les go to the beach while it's still sunny!

Knock knock.

Who's there?

Quiet Tina.

Quiet Tina who?

Quiet Tina Library! I'm trying to read!

Knock knock.

Who's there?

Vitamin.

Vitamin who?

Vitamin for the party!
He's a lot of fun!

Knock knock.

Who's there?

Tick.

Tick who?

Tick 'em up!
I'm a wobber!

Knock knock.

Who's there?

Orson.

Orson who?

**Orson cart will get us to school!
Should only take 5 hours!**

Knock knock.

Who's there?

Saul.

Saul who?

**Saul there is - there's none left!
Sorry! I ate it all!**

Knock knock.

Who's there?

Wilfred.

Wilfred who?

Wilfred be able to come out to play?

Knock knock.

Who's there?

Stopwatch.

Stopwatch who?

Stopwatch you're doing and let me in!

Knock knock.

Who's there?

Sharon.

Sharon who?

I'm Sharon my food with you. Would you like my broccoli?

Knock knock.

Who's there?

Rhino.

Rhino who?

Rhino all the funniest knock knock jokes! Here's another one!

Knock knock.

Who's there?

Hawaii.

Hawaii who?

Great thanks.
Hawaii you?

Knock knock.

Who's there?

Amish.

Amish who?

Amish you so much when I
don't see you!

Bonus Jokes!

Why did the girl throw her calendar out the window?

So the days would fly by!

Why did the man lose his job at the orange juice factory?

He didn't concentrate!

What has 3 horns and gives milk?

A cow on a motorbike!

What do you call a boy with
really short hair?
Shawn!

What is Tarzan's favorite
Christmas song?
Jungle bells, jungle bells!

Where do elephants go on holiday
in Italy?
Tusk-any!

How did the dentist get across
the harbor?

On the tooth ferry!

Which reindeer got into trouble for
not being polite?

Rude-olph!

What do you call your dad when
he is covered in snow?

Pop-sicle!

What do you call a grumpy cow?
MOOOO-dy!

What do you call a dinosaur that is very fussy about her food?
A Picky-saurus!

What did the doctor say when the nurse lost the scale?
No weigh!

Why couldn't the cross eyed teacher get a job?

She couldn't control her pupils!

What did the old tornado say to his wife?

**Let's twist again!
Like we did last summer!**

What do you call a Roman Emperorer with a cold?

Julius Sneezer!

Why do golfers wear 2 pairs of pants?
In case they get a hole in one!

Why was Mickey Mouse in trouble
at school?
He was being too Goofy!

Which rabbit brings Easter Eggs to
the fish in the sea?
The Oyster Bunny!

Why did the boy think he was very bright?
His dad called him 'Sun'!

What do you call a boy stuck to a wall?
Art!

What do you call a belt with a built in watch?
A waist of time!

Why did the robber lift weights at the gym?
To have buns of steal!

Why did the hummingbird always hum?
She forgot the words!

How do ghosts get their mail?
From the ghost office!

What do you call a dog who
has a fever?
A hot dog!

Where do all polar bears go to vote?
The North Poll!

Why did the skeleton always
miss the party?
He had no body to go with!

What did the girl wear to Disneyland?
Her Minnie skirt!

What do you call a really
nasty superhero?
Bratman!

Why is it so expensive to have
pet pelicans?
You get huge bills!

How do you talk to a chicken?
Use fowl language!

How did the clam call her friend?
On her shell phone!

What did one tomato say to the other tomato in the tomato race?
Ketchup!

Who wrote the famous book
'Salty Fish'?
Ann Chovie!

Why did the orange go to sea?
She was a naval orange!

What did the doctor say to the patient
who had a weird ringing in his ear?
Have you tried answering it?

What did the crab take when
it was sick?

Vitamin sea!

Why did the chemist keep on
telling jokes?

He was getting a good reaction!

What do really short kids do
after school?

Their gnome work!

Bonus
Knock Knock Jokes!

Knock knock.

Who's there?

Owl.

Owl who?

Owl be very happy when you finally open the door!

Knock knock.

Who's there?

Zany.

Zany who?

Zany body home today? Let me in!

Knock knock.

Who's there?

Waa.

Waa who?

You sure are excited considering all I did was knock!

Knock knock.

Who's there?

Soda.

Soda who?

Soda you want to let me in or what?

Knock knock.

Who's there?

Mabel.

Mabel who?

**Mabel works but yours
is broken.
Ha Ha!**

Knock knock.

Who's there?

Udder.

Udder who?

**Look Udder your shoe!
I think you stepped
in something!**

Knock knock.

Who's there?

Orange.

Orange who?

Orange you glad I finally made it?

Sorry I'm late!

Knock knock.

Who's there?

Troy.

Troy who?

Troy to answer quicker next time please!

Knock knock.

Who's there?

Turnip.

Turnip who?

**Turnip the music!
It's time to party!**

Knock knock.

Who's there?

Stork.

Stork who?

**Better stork up on candles
before the big storm!**

Knock knock.

Who's there?

Mandy.

Mandy who?

**Mandy lifeboats!
We're sinking!**

Knock knock.

Who's there?

Snow.

Snow who?

**Snow use asking me!
I'm 90 years old and can't
remember a thing!**

Knock knock.

Who's there?

Yukon.

Yukon who?

Yukon say that again!

Knock knock.

Who's there?

Four eggs.

Four eggs who?

Four eggs-ample why don't you get a doorbell?

Knock knock.

Who's there?

Matthew.

Matthew who?

**Matthew lace has come undone!
Noooo!**

Knock knock.

Who's there?

Patrick.

Patrick who?

**Patricked me into knocking
on your door!
Sorry!**

Knock knock.

Who's there?

Major.

Major who?

Major day with all these jokes, didn't I?

Knock knock.

Who's there?

Justin.

Justin who?

Justin time for dinner! Smells good!

Knock knock.

Who's there?

Fanny.

Fanny who?

Fanny body home?
Why don't you answer?

Knock knock.

Who's there?

Scott.

Scott who?

Scott nothing to do with you
my good sir!

Knock knock.

Who's there?

Jester.

Jester who?

Jester second!
Why are you in my house?

Knock knock.

Who's there?

Dishes.

Dishes who?

Dishes the police!
Open up!

Knock knock.

Who's there?

Zookeeper.

Zookeeper who?

Zookeeper way from my candy! I need it for my lunch tomorrow!

Knock knock.

Who's there?

Roxanne.

Roxanne who?

Roxanne pebbles make a really nice rock garden

Thank you!

.... so much for reading our book.

We hope you had lots of laughs and enjoyed these funny jokes.

We would appreciate it so much if you could leave us a review on Amazon. Reviews make a big difference and we appreciate your support. Thank you!

Our Joke Books are available as a series for all ages from 6-12.

To see our range of books or leave a review anytime please go to
FreddyFrost.com.

Thanks again!

Freddy Frost

.

Made in the USA
Monee, IL
11 December 2022

20927319R00066